American Horse Tales

North Shore

by Jennifer Camiccia

Penguin Workshop

For Ryan, Tina, and Melissa, and the fun we had on our weekly rides in Wailua. And to our beautiful horses that gave us so many wonderful memories—JC

PENGUIN WORKSHOP
An imprint of Penguin Random House LLC, New York

First published in the United States of America by Penguin Workshop, an imprint of Penguin Random House LLC, New York, 2021

Visit us online at penguinrandomhouse.com.

Library of Congress Control Number: 2021018937

Printed in the United States of America

ISBN 9780593225318 10 9 8 7 6 5 4 3 2 1 COMR

Chapter 1
Steer Undecorating

The announcer's voice boomed over the loudspeakers. "A big aloha to everyone this fine day, and welcome to the annual Hawai'i Women's Association Rodeo! Our next event in the main arena is steer undecorating—keiki division. Riders, take your places."

I followed Mom past the horse trailers to the outer gate. We were last on the list, and I could hear the other riders taking their turns. Sunshine nuzzled my shoulder as we waited, almost like she knew what was about to happen. My stomach felt like it did when I ate too much Spam musubi.

I breathed in the smells of the food trucks mixed with the sharp tang of cows. Sunshine nickered as we got closer to the arena. "I know, girl," I said. "It's exciting but kind of scary at the same time, huh?"

Sunshine's ear flicked forward. Sometimes, I really believed that she understood me.

A bell clanged to announce the next rider, and I finally became aware of Mom calling my name. "It's time, Starley," Mom said excitedly, holding Sunshine so I could mount up. "No matter what happens, I'm proud of you."

"Thanks, Mom," I said, and tipped my hat to her.

I sat in the saddle and squeezed my legs together to urge Sunshine forward. Mom blew me a kiss and stepped back so Sunshine and I could walk past.

The announcer talked over the music still playing. "Our last contender in the keiki division comes from the north shore and is from a long line of cowboys, or—as we call them in Hawai'i—paniolos. Let's make some noise for Starley Robinson."

The crowd clapped and cheered. I felt Sunshine's muscles bunch beneath my legs. She was getting ready, and so was I. My thumb brushed over the raised silver belt buckle Tutu had given me this morning. My grandmother had won first place in the keiki division when she was ten. *Now it's my turn,* I thought. *I can't let her down.*

I nodded to the man who was wearing a western shirt and waiting for my signal. The steer bellowed in the pen, the metal gate clanking as it opened. The steer took off running. In seconds, it passed the first pole. The man holding the rope in front of Sunshine dropped it with a shout.

I squeezed my legs and leaned forward, my eyes glued to the steer running across the arena. My stomach didn't have a chance to catch up to my body as Sunshine lunged forward. The hazer—the other rider that kept the steer running straight—guided the steer toward the middle of the arena.

I nudged Sunshine, asking her to go even faster. The bright pink ribbon on the steer's shoulder was all I focused on. I gripped the reins in my right hand and urged Sunshine closer to the ribbon—closer to winning.

Everything we'd trained for came down to this moment. My braid bounced against my back, and I could hear the hazer calling to the steer. Her shouts kept the steer running in the right direction.

I pointed the reins forward, and Sunshine raced toward the steer. One hand gripped the horn as I leaned to the side. *The bright pink ribbon is so close!* I reached for it, my fingers brushing the silky material before I wrapped my hand around it and pulled.

The ribbon didn't come off right away, so I tugged harder. This time it pulled loose, and I quickly raised my hand straight over my head.

A buzzer sounded loudly. The crowd cheered even louder.

Sunshine trotted to the side of the arena. Mom beamed at me as they announced my time.

Six seconds! The fastest time for my division and my personal best! The blood in my veins rushed, and it felt like I was still in the ring, galloping with Sunshine.

"You did it, honey!" Mom danced through the gate and waited for me to dismount before she scooped me into a giant hug. "I'm so proud of you."

I laughed and danced with Mom in my own mixture of running in place and straight-up jumping. Mom laughed and snapped her fingers together. Mom couldn't dance without snapping—something my older sister, Megan, and I loved to tease her about.

"Congratulations on a spectacular ride," said a woman's voice behind me.

When I turned, I could barely believe who stood there. *It's Maria González!* She had on a battered black cowboy hat, pulled over her dark curls, and red boots that matched her lipstick.

Maria smiled. "That was some pretty spectacular riding. I bet you could outride most adults."

I wondered with embarrassment, *How long did my mouth hang open before I remembered to close it?* "Um . . . thank you," I said. I couldn't believe *the* Maria González was standing in front of me, complimenting my riding! I realized she was still talking, and I forced myself to tune back in.

"Is that something you might be interested in?" Maria asked, her gaze swinging between Mom and me.

Mom smiled at me. She seemed to be waiting for me to answer, only I wasn't sure what the question was.

"What do you think?" I asked Mom, hoping she'd clear it up for me.

Mom hiked her purse higher on her shoulder. "I think it's something we should talk about as a family. It's a very generous offer, Miss González. Thank you for thinking of Starley."

Maria reached into her back pocket and pulled out a small card. "Here's my cell number and email. Give me a call when you've all had a chance to talk. I'll need an answer by next week."

My curiosity soared, and I wondered what she needed an answer to. *Why wasn't I listening instead of daydreaming?* I couldn't wait to get Mom alone so I could ask her, only I didn't want Maria to leave. *When will I ever get a chance to talk to someone who can ride like her?*

"I'm so sorry," Mom said, pointing to where Dad, Tutu, and Megan were standing. "I see my family waiting for us."

Maria held out her hand to me. "Of course! It was a delight to meet you, Starley. I'll be cheering for you later this afternoon, when you get your prize at the closing ceremony."

Her hand was rough and lined with calluses, and her strong fingers squeezed mine. I smiled with pure gladness. *This day can't get any better*, I thought as I watched her walk away.

Chapter 2
The Offer

Megan ran to me with wide eyes. "Did you get to talk to her?"

I nodded, my smile growing even bigger. I could tell Megan was impressed by the way she tossed her perfectly curled hair and tried not to smile.

Dad stepped in between us and hugged me so tight, I gasped. I laughed as he twirled me around. "My daughter, the superstar rodeo queen."

"Let me see her, Howard," Tutu commanded,

holding on to Sunshine's bridle with the confidence of someone used to horses. She handed me the reins. "A responsible cowgirl always takes care of her horse before herself. You did good out there, keiki, but it's not only about you, yeah?"

I bowed my head. For the last few minutes, I'd forgotten about Sunshine. I vowed silently to make sure I gave her extra treats to show her how much I loved her.

"Yes, Tutu," I said. "You're right."

"Of course I am," Tutu said with a snort. She sounded almost like a horse for one second, and I struggled not to laugh.

Megan must have thought the same thing, because she giggled and said, "You totally sounded like Sunshine, Tutu."

Tutu frowned, and Megan stopped mid-giggle. Tutu was pretty much the only person who scared Megan. "Just remember, you two, anything worthwhile in life has to be earned with hard work and patience."

"Yes, Tutu," I said, even though I wasn't sure I believed her. Dad and Mom worked really hard, especially lately. But they were always worried about money and stressed out all the time.

"Why don't I take a picture with Starley and Tutu next to Sunshine?" Megan asked, holding up her phone and sounding as sweet as maple syrup. "You know, so we can have a memory of this special day."

My parents and Tutu agreed, and we spent the next ten minutes taking "memory pictures."

When my stomach growled, Dad chuckled. "How about we all help you groom Sunshine? After that, we can go hit up the food trucks."

"Thanks, Dad," I said, my mouth watering as I

thought about kālua-pork sliders.

"Sounds like a wonderful idea!" Mom said. "I could use something to drink."

"What did Maria González want, Mom?" I asked. "I was sort of too excited to hear what she said."

"I thought you seemed unusually quiet," Mom replied, with a smile. "We can talk about it while you girls groom the horse."

I quickly unbuckled Sunshine's saddle. Megan helped me lift it off and place it on the sawhorse next to us. I grabbed two curry combs and handed one to Megan.

"Maria invited Starley to the horse camp she runs the last two weeks in June," Mom said. "She was impressed with Starley's riding and wants to mentor her. She even offered a scholarship."

Dad's eyes widened, and Megan grinned.

The curry comb dropped right out of my hand

with a soft thunk onto the solid, packed red dirt. "I've always wanted to go, but you said it was way too expensive! I can't believe this! Can I go? Can I?"

Tutu picked up the comb and started to brush Sunshine's sweaty coat. "You know my father worked as a paniolo on the Big Island. He taught me to ride before I could walk, and he'd be so proud of Starley. I think this is a wonderful opportunity for her."

Maria wants to mentor me? I could only imagine how much I could learn. This was my chance to work toward my dream of being a professional rodeo rider!

"Yes. But two weeks is a long time," Mom said. "Starley wouldn't know anyone."

"You went away to camp when you were her age," Tutu reminded her. "We could always visit on the weekends. It's only an hour-and-a-half drive."

I smiled at Tutu. I knew she would understand

how important this was to me.

Mom nodded, and I could tell she liked the idea of visiting me.

Dad cleared his throat and looked at me with a serious expression. "Two weeks is longer than you've ever been away from home."

"Please, Daddy," I begged. "I'll be fine, and I really want to go!"

Dad looked at Mom, and she gave a little nod. "We'll talk about it," he said, but his grin told me the answer was yes.

I ran over and hugged Dad and then Mom. "Thank you so much. I can't believe this is happening!"

Mom laughed. "It's not decided yet," she teased.

"Hooey," Tutu said. "Put the girl out of her misery already."

"We still need to figure out the details . . ." Mom

tapped a finger to her chin like she was in deep thought.

Dad chuckled at my hopeful expression. "Okay. I think we've teased her enough. You can go, little star."

Sunshine whinnied, and I quickly ran back to her side. "Did you hear that, girl? We're going to Maria's horse camp!"

Dad's smile faltered. "I'm not sure Sunshine can go with you. We'll need to ask Mr. Griffin. He was nice enough to let you ride her in the rodeo. I'm not sure what he'll say about her going with you for two weeks."

I hugged Sunshine's neck. "But I can't go without her!"

"You might have to," Mom said gently.

"Why can't we just buy Sunshine from Mr. Griffin?" I asked, even though I knew the answer.

Money. Or, in our case, not having enough of it. That was why we sponsored Sunshine instead of owning her.

Dad rubbed the back of his neck. "You know the answer to that, little star."

"Don't be a brat," Megan said. "Mom and Dad pay grouchy Mr. Griffin every month for you to sponsor Sunshine. It's better than not having a horse at all."

I hung my head. Megan was right. "I'm sorry," I whispered. I loosened my arms and let them fall. Sunshine snuffled my hands looking for treats. She trusted me, and I trusted her. That was why I couldn't just wait for Mom and Dad to save enough to buy her. I would have to do it myself.

Chapter 3
The Perfect Plan

The next day, Mom and Dad filled out the online forms for Maria's horse camp. When they were done, I looked at the website while I ate my breakfast. It promised to make me the best rodeo rider in Hawaiʻi, maybe even the whole United States.

I would need to be the best if I wanted my idea to work.

My plan was simple: Phase one, Maria would teach me all her tricks, which would then make me the best rider in my age division. Phase two, I'd win the Hilo rodeo. Phase three, I'd buy Sunshine.

The prize in the youth division was five thousand bucks. That should be enough to buy Sunshine. Then I'd never have to be away from her again.

Mom peered over my shoulder at the picture of smiling boys and girls. "They look so happy."

My smile slipped. Horses were easy. Horses I could talk to. But other kids my age? That was harder. "What if the other campers don't like me?"

Mom shook her head. "Impossible! How could anyone not like you? Just be yourself."

"I have so many things I could say to that," Megan said, strolling into the kitchen and grabbing a banana. "But since I'm late, I'll let it go." She flashed me a teasing smile before turning to Mom. "Ready? I don't want to be even later."

Mom nodded and scooped up her keys. She

tilted her head as she considered me. "We'll talk more when I get back."

"Okay." I glanced out the back window to where the overgrown grass of our backyard met the pasture we shared with Mr. Griffin. Four horses grazed in the distance. I spotted Sunshine easily. Her chestnut coat gleamed in the afternoon sun. She lifted her head up and looked in my direction, almost like she knew I was thinking about her.

Tutu pushed the sliding door open and walked in from the garden. She held up a handful of carrots. "You can take these to the horses when you're pau with breakfast."

I nodded. I watched as she rinsed off the rest of the dirt. "Tutu, would you help me ask Mr. Griffin if I could bring Sunshine with me to camp?"

Tutu sniffed. "That old grouch? You'd do better without me."

"Please," I pleaded. "He sort of scares me."

"He's full of hot air," Tutu grumbled. "I never heard anyone talk story as much as he does."

"Maybe if I take him Mom's banana bread, he'll say yes," I said.

Tutu opened the back door. "Come on, then. Better get it over with, yeah?"

I pushed away my half-eaten oatmeal and hopped down from my stool at the counter. Scooping up the container of banana bread, I hurried after Tutu. She pumped both arms as she darted around mud puddles and our half-finished driveway.

Mr. Griffin's dark wood gate opened quietly. Tutu marched down the pretty walkway lined with bright red hibiscus and purple bougainvillea.

Mr. Griffin opened the door before we reached the front porch. "If it isn't my two favorite Robinsons," he called out. "To what do I owe the pleasure?"

Tutu held out her hand to me. I took it, glad for the tight clasp of her fingers in mine. "Starley would like to ask you something," she said, squeezing my fingers gently.

I opened my mouth and then closed it. *What should I say?*

"Any day now," Mr. Griffin said with raised brows.

"Give her a second." Tutu looked down at me patiently. She didn't try to talk for me. She insisted I'd never get over my shyness if Mom and Dad always butted in when my voice froze.

I thrust the tin of banana bread at him.

"Well, thank you, young lady. I do love banana bread. It reminds me of the time my older daughter made me the best banana-cream pie in the history of these great islands—"

"Yes, I'm sure she did," Tutu interrupted easily.

"Starley, ask your question."

"Can I please take Sunshine—"

"Can't hear you." Mr. Griffin turned his head so his right ear faced me. "Speak up."

Tutu squeezed my fingers but said nothing.

I cleared my throat and thought about Sunshine. "Can I please take Sunshine to a horse camp with me for two weeks?"

I held my breath and studied the way his bushy white eyebrows wiggled as he wrinkled his forehead. *Please let him say yes.*

"I'm sorry, girly. I know how partial you are to my Sunshine, but she's too valuable to let out of my sight for two weeks." He scratched the thick mustache that matched his eyebrows.

"It's a ranch in Mākaha," I said, the words galloping out of me like if I said them fast enough, he might change his mind. "Maria González runs it. She's famous! You must have heard of her. That's where Sunshine would be. I promise I wouldn't let anything happen to her."

"I have *not* heard of her," he said. "But that wouldn't sway me, even if I had. You take good care of Sunshine, and she's fond of you. I do appreciate you riding her for me. But you wouldn't want our agreement to stop because you won't take no for an answer, would you?"

Tutu tucked my hand even more firmly in hers. "Is that your final answer?" Tutu asked, sounding like the guy in the game show she watched every afternoon.

"It is," Mr. Griffin said with a firm nod.

I followed Tutu out the gate and down Mr. Griffin's perfect driveway, then up our bumpy one with weeds everywhere. I kicked a rock, hard. My big toe throbbed afterward, but I didn't care.

"I'm sorry," Tutu said once we were back inside our kitchen.

My oatmeal had turned lumpy and cold. I put it in the sink and filled the bowl up with hot water. "It's okay." But it didn't feel okay.

Tutu ran a soothing hand down my long braid. "I'm proud of how you spoke up for what you wanted," she said. "I know it was difficult for you."

"It didn't make any difference." I shrugged and looked out the window to where Sunshine grazed. She trusted me.

I *had* to go to Maria's camp—even without Sunshine. It was the only way I could get good enough to win the money I needed.

"It's just for two weeks. You'll be back before you know it, and Sunshine will be right here waiting for you." Tutu placed a kiss on the top of my head and then headed to her room.

I slid the back door open and ran barefoot out to the wire fence that butted Mr. Griffin's pasture. I was careful to stay on the cool crabgrass and avoid the pincher leaves of the hilahila weeds.

Sunshine trotted to greet me. She smiled and tossed her head. I plucked a handful of the taller grass, and she nibbled daintily at the ends.

Sunshine sniffed my hand, her soft brown eyes watching me. "I won't be gone long. There's no reason to be worried, okay?"

Dad always said if you make a promise, it's sacred. It's not something you should say unless you really mean it. I gently rubbed the soft part of her muzzle. "I promise," I whispered.

Her ears flicked back and forth to let me know she was listening.

Chapter 4

Horse Camp

I zipped the jacket my mom insisted I bring. The weather here in the mountains was colder than I was used to. Green hills rolled right to the base of the mountain. Peacocks cawed, and their noise mixed with the lower groans of cattle.

The ranch had a big, green barn with smaller outbuildings surrounding it in a circle. Horses grazed lazily in the pasture. There were six other campers around my age. Three girls on my left giggled and chattered. Three boys lounged against the barn wall like they were bored. They all seemed to know one another. I overheard one of the girls say that this was her second time at camp.

Maria clapped her hands, each of her short nails painted a different color. "Welcome back, campers. Most of you have been here before. Let me introduce you to our newest horse specialist."

She held out her hand to me. "This is Starley Robinson. I recruited her after she won first prize in the steer-undecorating competition in the Wai'anae rodeo. She's an impressive rider, and I think you can all learn something from her. Who here is excited to show Starley the ropes?"

A boy with short, spiky hair shook his head and muttered something under his breath. His hand went up, but he somehow managed to look like he didn't care if he raised it or not. A girl with red hair and light brown skin also raised her hand. She looked over at me with a welcoming smile.

Maria smiled approvingly. "Excellent! Thank you, Heidi and Liko. I've assigned her Pilikia to ride. I think she's up for the challenge."

Liko smiled at Heidi, and she rolled her eyes. The other kids started whispering. Maria ignored them and smiled at me. "I'm so happy you're here, Starley. I think you're going to really shine."

A warm glow filled me. I tried my best to not grin like Sunshine when I fed her sugar cubes.

"Starley, the others know my teaching style. You'll have to learn as we go. First, I want you to put the idea of fun right out of your head," Maria said, her friendly smile taking the edge off of her words. "This camp is not about fun. It's about making you the best. We rodeo riders are the true horsemen. We ride our horses to the limit, and then we ask them to give us a little more. Do you think you have it in you to ride like nothing else is as important as that prize?"

All eyes looked at me, waiting for my answer. I gave a small nod.

"You can do better than that!" Maria clapped her hands hard. "What do you say, campers: Is winning the most important thing?"

"Yes!" the rest of the campers shouted.

"Yes!" I said, not quite a shout but louder than usual. My stomach fizzed like a soda that had been shaken up and opened too fast. This was definitely the best day of my life.

I followed behind Liko and Heidi as they walked inside the barn. "Maria must think you're a pretty great rider," Heidi called over her shoulder. "Pilikia can act wild."

"Or Maria's testing her." Liko strode down the

middle of the barn and stopped outside a stall. "This is the famous Pilikia. You know what that means in Hawaiian, right?"

"Trouble," I answered, a knot starting to form in the middle of my stomach.

"Huh," Liko grunted. "I didn't think a haole girl like you would know Hawaiian."

"I was born here," I said softly. "And my tutu is Hawaiian."

Unlike Megan, I didn't care if people called me haole. Tutu told me the word really means "newcomer," but over time it's come to mean any white person. And with my light brown hair and blue eyes, I didn't look like I had any Hawaiian at all.

Heidi pushed in front of Liko and held her palm flat. In the middle was a perfect white cube. "Pilikia loves sugar. Don't you, boy?"

A dark brown horse with a black, silky mane

nuzzled Heidi's palm. He stared past Heidi to me. It was like he was waiting to meet me. "Hey, there," I said, moving my hand slowly so he could sniff it. "You're a beauty, aren't you?"

Liko shoved both hands into his pockets. "I wanted to ride him this year," he said.

Pilikia snuffled my hand and then turned his attention back to Heidi. "Sorry," I said to the horse. "I'm sugarless. Next time, I'll bring some."

"Sugarless," Heidi said with a giggle. "Like a piece of gum?"

I hadn't meant to be funny. I hated how my face always turned red at the worst times. I looked away, hoping they wouldn't notice.

A high-pitched bell interrupted whatever Heidi was about to say next. She tilted her head and hooked a thumb toward the door. "Time to go to the dorms."

Liko nodded to me. "See you around," he said before heading out of the barn.

I followed Heidi as she headed away from him. "You're going to love it here," she said. "Wait until you meet my horse, Mango. She's a paint pony, and she's the sweetest. Do you have a horse at home?"

I nodded. It wasn't really a lie. Sunshine and I belonged to each other. "Her name is Sunshine."

Heidi pushed open the door to one of the small cabins on the right. "Cool name. Why didn't you bring her?"

I ducked my head and tried to think of a good reason. "Um . . ."

"Parents said no?" she guessed. "My parents didn't let me bring Mango last year. They said it was too much work to ship her, since we live on Maui."

I nodded. My parents *did* say I couldn't bring Sunshine. I would tell Heidi later that I didn't actually own my horse, but now didn't seem like the right time.

"Too bad. But you'll do fine." Heidi grinned and put her arm through mine. "I can tell we're going to be friends."

I didn't even care about my red face. I had a friend. It was a good start.

Chapter 5
Bunking Up

After orientation, a teenage girl named Lisa showed us to our room. She pointed to a bunk against the wall. "You're on the bottom," she said to me. She nodded to Heidi. "And you get top." She pointed to the next two and told them where they were sleeping.

"I don't like sleeping up high," one of the girls said with a high-pitched whine. "My mom wrote a letter saying I didn't have to this time."

"Sorry," Lisa said. "Maria was very clear. You can't switch, and I suggest you don't complain. She's kicked people out for less. I'm sure you remember Leilani from last year."

All the girls stopped their grumbling. "Settle in and let me know if you need anything," Lisa called out as she left.

I sat on the edge of my bunk. The excitement of earlier had worn off with the finality of Lisa's voice. *Would Maria really kick people out of camp for complaining? And why does she care where we sleep?*

"Just when I thought Maria couldn't get meaner," Heidi said. Her short, curly red hair framed her face like cotton candy.

The other girls sat on the opposite bunk.

"I'm Pumai," said the girl afraid of heights. She had wide brown eyes, with the thickest lashes I'd ever seen.

"And I'm Kristina," the other girl said. She had long, straight brown hair pulled up in a high ponytail and gray eyes. "Which event did you win?"

"Steer undecorating," I replied, the backs of my legs pushed against the metal frame of the bed. "What about you?"

"Barrel racing," Pumai answered.

"Barrel racing," Kristina said and high-fived Pumai. "I beat the boys' time in my division. I guess that wasn't good enough to get Maria to give me a scholarship, though."

No one is supposed to know about the scholarship! My cheeks burned.

"There were scholarships?" Pumai asked with narrowed eyes. "Who got one?"

Heidi looked from Kristina to me. "I guess Starley did. That's cool. Good for you, Starley."

"Doesn't mean you're the best." Kristina

narrowed her eyes at me like she was daring me to argue.

I folded my arms across my chest like I'd seen Megan do when she was giving my mom attitude. I heard myself say, "I guess we'll see."

My ears burned, and my fingers tingled. *I can't believe I said that to Kristina!*

"I guess we will," Kristina echoed with a wide smile.

"It's not a contest," Heidi said to Kristina. "We need to be a team, remember?"

Kristina sniffed. "There's no team in a rodeo. Just the rider and their horse."

Pumai pulled a stuffed horse out of her backpack.

Kristina giggled. "Speaking of horses . . . do you really still sleep with that? Aren't you a little too old?"

I thought about the small square of silk tucked

inside my suitcase. I'd never slept without it. But there was no way I was going to let Kristina see it and make fun of me.

Pumai hugged her stuffed horse tight and set it carefully on her pillow. "I'll never outgrow it. You're just jealous."

Kristina frowned, and Heidi turned her attention to unpacking. I stared a second too long, and Kristina narrowed her eyes and focused on me. "Whatchu looking at?"

I lowered my head and unzipped my suitcase. My stomach hurt, and I wished Megan were here so I could ask her advice on what to say next. She always knew what to do.

Kristina stomped across the room and tossed her suitcase next to a dresser. "I get the top drawers," she bit out. I wasn't sure why she was angry.

I kept my head down and rushed to the

bathroom. It smelled like pee. A cockroach scurried across the floor and ran behind the toilet. I kept an eye on it while I brushed my teeth.

"You stay over there," I said, with a mouthful of toothpaste. "I won't bug you if you don't bug me. Get it?" I snorted, and half my toothpaste landed on the mirror.

Heidi was already asleep when I climbed into bed. Kristina and Pumai watched me as I slipped under the covers.

"Can't wait to see how you ride tomorrow," Kristina said, somehow making it sound like a threat.

Pumai turned over and faced the wall. I closed my eyes tight. I wished I were in my soft bed with Megan snoring next door.

I couldn't wait until the morning. I'd show them why Maria chose me.

Chapter 6
Pilikia

The horse I was assigned stared at me and rolled his eyes. “Not you, too,” I whispered. I held out my hand for Pilikia to sniff and then rubbed the soft spot of his nose. It was Sunshine’s favorite place to be scratched.

This horse just snorted. He was clearly not impressed with me.

“Pilikia is a champion,” Maria said, slapping the horse’s neck. “He lives up to his name, so watch out.”

Kristina waited for her to be out of earshot. "You know why she's letting you ride him, right?" She brushed the blond mane of the beautiful palomino she'd brought with her from home.

"Because she thinks I'm a good rider," I said, trying to sound confident.

Kristina smirked. "She wants you to fail. That horse is out of control."

Pumai giggled. She led her horse—a gray-and-white spotted horse with a lively step—past Kristina and tied her to the post. "Sorry, Starley. I hope you don't get hurt."

I scrambled for something to say. "Maybe he's like my friend's horse, Molasses. Her name makes you think she's slow, but she's actually really fast."

"And maybe Pilikia is a sweet horse instead of a troublemaker?" Kristina asked with a smirk.

Heidi rolled her eyes. "Don't listen to them,

Starley. I'm sure you'll be able to handle him."

Heidi walked her horse closer to Kristina's. She reached out her hand to pat the palomino's neck. "Butterscotch sure is beautiful," she said to Kristina.

"Well, she *is* a thoroughbred," Kristina said with a sniff. "Which makes her better than most horses."

Heidi's eyes narrowed. "That's not true!"

"Is there a problem, girls?" Maria asked, walking past Mango and grabbing hold of Pilikia's bridle.

"No problem," Kristina said with wide, innocent eyes. "Just introducing our horses to one another. Isn't Heidi's horse sweet?"

Maria frowned as she studied us. "Remember that you need to work together for the next two weeks. I won't have any disunity. It's not good for the horses."

Kristina smiled. "Of course."

Heidi gritted her teeth. "Yes, Maria."

"This is for you, Starley." Maria handed me a small leather crop. "Pilikia can be a handful, so you might need it."

I flipped it around in my hands with a small grimace. "I don't use these."

Maria's lip lifted on one side. "Oh, I'm sorry. I didn't know you were in charge."

I clutched the crop tightly. "I didn't—"

"Not only will you use it, but you will use it as much as I say." Maria narrowed her eyes at me until I nodded. She walked back over to where two of the boys in the group were getting ready to mount.

"Wow," Kristina said. "I guess we don't have to worry about you being the teacher's pet anymore."

"I don't like using crops, either," Heidi said in a low voice. "But Maria says it's part of learning how to train a horse. We don't have a choice."

Pumai put her foot in the stirrup and swung up.

"You don't have to hurt the horse. It's just for show."

I clasped it close to my leg. "I guess I can just hold it."

"Just wait until she makes you wear spurs," Kristina said.

"Spurs? No way." I shook my head back and forth. I'd heard that some rodeo riders said it was the only way to make sure a horse listened. But the thought of hurting a horse, any horse, made my stomach ache.

"It's for show," Heidi reassured me. "No worries."

The girls all waited for me to get on Pilikia. The three boys were already in the middle of the arena with Maria and Lisa.

I put my foot in the stirrup, and Pilikia shuffled sideways. I hopped as fast as I could on one foot while the horse bared his teeth and grinned at me. *Great, now even the horse is making fun of me.*

Kristina giggled. "And you're the rider we're supposed to learn things from?"

My face burned. I grabbed the horn on the front of the saddle to steady myself as I tried again. This time, I was nearly in the saddle when Pilikia turned abruptly and shook me right off his back.

I hit the ground so hard, I bounced on my ʻōkole. My teeth ached where they'd slammed together. My fingers curled against the loose dirt beneath me.

"Get up!" Liko shouted from the arena. "Before Pilikia steps on you."

I rolled to my knees and lurched to a standing position. Maria stared over at me. *Does she regret giving me a scholarship?*

Heidi jumped off her horse and grabbed Pilikia's reins. "I got him. Go ahead and get on."

I didn't want to. I missed Sunshine. She would never do this. I glared at Pilikia before I picked the crop off the ground. Maybe it wouldn't be so bad to use it. Some horses might need it.

"Okay," Maria said when I finally joined them in the arena. "Shake it off. We all have bad moments. A winner doesn't let those bad moments define them. Do you want to be a winner?"

"Yes," I said, my voice melding with the others'.

"Say it!" she instructed.

"We want to be winners!"

Chapter 7
Just Listen

Pilikia finally settled down. I kept the crop close to my leg. I couldn't use it—it just didn't feel right. I watched as Maria insisted Heidi use her crop when Mango refused to walk around the barrels.

Heidi's shoulders slumped, and her lips trembled.

Kristina clenched her jaw, but even she said nothing. I pleaded silently to Pilikia to listen to my commands. I didn't know what I'd do if he didn't.

Will I use the crop? My stomach cramped and twisted.

"Is this what you call riding?" Maria shouted, her cheeks red. "I can't teach you if you won't listen."

Pumai wiped at her eyes and sniffed. Kristina's feelings were harder to read. Liko shook his head, and the other two boys frowned.

I squeezed my legs together slightly. Pilikia trotted, and then he went from a trot to a smooth canter. We moved around the course faster and faster until my hair whipped my cheeks. *Is he faster than Sunshine?* Maybe. But he wasn't as obedient. Halfway through the course, he decided he'd had enough and stopped so fast, I nearly sailed over his head.

"Use your crop!" Maria shouted to me. "Now!"

I held it up so he could see it and hoped that gesture would be enough. He just tossed his head and chomped on the bit. I used all the tricks I knew.

But he just wouldn't move.

"Is there a reason you're not listening?" Maria asked me. She wasn't shouting anymore. The stillness in her words made them even scarier. "Use. The. Crop."

I held it out. The black leather gleamed in the sunlight. My arm dropped to my side like it wasn't attached to me. *This is Maria González.* She was a champion. *Why do I think I know more than she does?* But it didn't matter how much she knew or how mad she'd be. I just couldn't do it.

"I'm sorry," I said, looking down at Pilikia's mane.

"Don't apologize to me," Maria said, riding up closer. Then with a quick dart of her hand, she slapped her crop across Pilikia's tender flanks.

One second I was in the saddle. The next I was on my back in the dirt. I stared up at the clouds. My head hurt. My ʻōkole hurt. My back throbbed.

A hand reached out, and Liko pulled me up. "Don't listen to her. I think you're brave," he said in a low voice.

My cheeks felt as red as Maria's lipstick.

"When you're done resting," Maria said, "please get back on your mount."

I didn't want to get back on. I wanted Sunshine. I wanted my mom. I missed my family with an ache worse than the one on my ʻōkole.

"I'll help," Liko said. "She'll get really mad if you don't."

I gritted my teeth against the stiffness of my legs. "Okay."

Once I was back on, Liko whispered something to Pilikia, his low voice calming the horse. I gently ran my hand across his side. "Sorry, boy. Please just listen, okay?"

It was as if Pilikia understood me. Or maybe he

just didn't want to be hit again. Whatever the reason, he obeyed. Maria's shouts all blended together for me. I tuned her out and used my instincts.

"Good work, everyone," Maria said with a clap of her hands. "You're all well on your way to excellence. Who wants to be a winner?"

"I do," we all said, but this time the excitement seemed dim, like it was hidden underneath a huge pile of horse manure.

Chapter 8
Wake-Up Call

After we finished riding and getting cleaned up, it was time for dinner. I held my tray and listened as Heidi described each dish in detail.

"The lomi lomi salmon is delicious, and the kālua pig is so ʻono. I don't see chicken long rice, but they'll definitely have it another night." Heidi took a heaping spoonful of white sticky rice and dumped it on my plate.

I wondered what Mom and Dad were eating. I

pictured Megan making a face at all the carbs they served here. I missed my sister, even if she was annoying. And I really missed my parents and Tutu.

I scratched at the tiny red bumps all over my arm. I bet they washed their sheets with the kind of laundry detergent I was allergic to.

Heidi sat next to Liko. He moved over to make room for us. I bit my lip as I eased down on the hard wooden bench. My tailbone still hurt from falling off Pilikia.

"I don't think you met Greg and Evan." Liko pointed to the other two boys.

I lifted my chin in greeting to both boys. "I think I saw you at a rodeo," I said to Evan. "You were roping steer."

Evan grunted and shoveled a forkful of kālua pig and rice into his mouth.

"So, how do you like Pilikia?" Greg asked. He

had a sly grin on his face.

I shrugged. I nibbled on the rice and wrinkled my nose. It was way too salty.

"You're going to have to use the crop sooner or later if you want to be a rodeo rider," Greg said. "All the good riders use them."

"Maybe you wouldn't fall if you did," Evan muttered.

"She'll get the hang of it," Heidi said. "Everyone falls sometimes."

I put my fork down. I knew Heidi was sticking up for me, but my face burned as I imagined what everyone thought. They must wonder why Maria picked me for a scholarship. I blinked quickly. *I can't cry in front of them!*

A hand landed on my shoulder. I looked up at Maria's smiling face. "Hey, there, my champion. I just wanted to come by and tell you not to feel bad about today. I'm sure all of your friends can tell you what it was like for them last year. You'll get the hang of things. And starting tomorrow, I'm going to have you doing drills. You thought you were fast before? I'll teach you to get the most out of your horse! Sound good?"

I nodded. Her words felt like a hug just when I needed it. I pushed away the memory of her shouting and focused on the friendly smile she was giving me now. And—like Greg had said—lots of riders used crops. They couldn't *all* be wrong.

Maria was a ten-time champion, and I was just a nobody. But with her help, I could be a champion, too. I'd win the Hilo rodeo and be able to buy Sunshine. That's what I needed to concentrate on: Sunshine.

I went back to my food and tried the lomi lomi salmon. It was even saltier than the rice, but that was okay. Lomi lomi salmon was always salty, so I expected it. I ate and listened to the others tease one another and laugh. I didn't belong yet, but that was okay, too.

Maria promised that I'd get the hang of it.

That night, the wind sounded like a woman crying. I huddled beneath my blankets, eyes wide open, heart beating faster and faster.

"It's Pele, the goddess of the volcano," Heidi whispered loud enough for me to hear. "She roams the island calling for her lost love."

I didn't answer. If I was quiet, then maybe Heidi would think I was asleep and stop talking. The wind howled even louder. I squeezed my eyes shut and thought about why I was here. I wanted to learn about horses and be the best I could be. Even though I missed my own bed and Sunshine, this was my chance for an adventure. And really, the wind sounded a lot like the wind back home. The rain against the roof was as familiar to me as Tutu singing me a lullaby. I drifted to sleep missing home, but also excited about what tomorrow would bring.

The air felt heavy, like it was about to rain. I was riding Sunshine in my pasture back at home, but I don't remember how I got there. All of a sudden, Sunshine tossed her head and bolted toward the fence. It was too high to jump. "Sunshine, stop!" I cried, pulling her reins.

"It's not Sunshine," Maria shouted. She balanced on top of the fence with her arms folded across her chest. "Pilikia is your horse now. He only listens to winners, and you will never be a winner."

I pulled the reins harder. "Please, Pilikia," I begged. "You'll hurt yourself."

But no matter how hard I pulled, or how much I pleaded, Pilikia didn't listen. He crashed into the fence, and the sky split open.

When I blinked my eyes open the next morning, soft sunlight streamed in through the slatted window blinds. The wind had died down, and all I could hear were the snores from across the room.

I put on my riding clothes and sniffed away my tears. I tried to focus on my plan and not think about the nightmare. I needed Maria's help to be the best rodeo rider ever. I couldn't let anything distract me.

All I needed to do was to show Pilikia who was boss. Maria said he wouldn't respect me until he knew I was in charge. I gripped my crop and stomped toward the barn. *I can do this. I can do this.*

If I repeated it enough, maybe it would come true.

Chapter 9

Here Comes Sunshine

"If he doesn't listen, then give him a swat on his flank," Maria ordered.

I wanted to take the crop and throw it onto the ground. I wanted to scream and shout. But I couldn't. I couldn't if I wanted my plan to work. Phase one: Learn all Maria had to teach so I could be a champion.

My body itched like a million mosquitoes had snacked on me all night long. My ʻōkole and legs throbbed from being tossed off Pilikia. But none of that seemed to matter when I thought about using the crop. *Can I be the best rodeo rider if I don't?*

There was a commotion by the fence. Maria shaded her eyes with her hand. "I think you have company, Starley."

I turned and saw my sister waving both hands over her head like she was directing airplanes. *What is she doing here?* I smiled and waved back.

"Hey, Starley! Guess what?" Megan called.

Liko and Evan both stared with their eyes bugging out. Greg grinned and walked over to her with all the confidence of a ten-year-old.

"Howzit," he said, tilting his chin up.

Megan ignored him. "We brought Sunshine," she continued with a wide grin. "Mom and Dad are unloading her as we speak."

My mouth dropped open. I couldn't believe it!

"Isn't Sunshine your horse?" Heidi asked. "That's awesome!"

I ran and hugged Megan. She patted my back before untangling my arms. "Okay, okay. You know my rule about hugs."

"Never in public," I said with a grin. I was too happy to even care about Megan's stupid rule.

Maria dismounted and walked over. "Surprise! I was thrilled when your parents called me yesterday. I know how much you must be missing Sunshine."

"I can't believe she's really here!" I jumped up and down, barely able to contain my excitement.

"Go ahead to the barn and get that horse of yours." Maria smiled and waved her hands in the direction of the barn. "Tell your parents to leave the paperwork with Lisa at the front desk."

Megan hooked her arm in mine. "Race you!"

Racing while holding on to Megan's arm wasn't a

real race at all. I laughed when she tried to trip me. Not even her normal tricks could make me mad.

"How did Mom and Dad talk Mr. Griffin into letting Sunshine come?" I asked when we slowed to a walk at the barn's entrance.

Megan waggled her eyebrows up and down. "Mom made him a lasagna, and Dad offered to do his taxes for him for the next two years for free."

Mom was tightening Sunshine's saddle when we walked inside. I ran to her and threw my arms around her waist. "I missed you!"

She kissed the top of my head. "We missed you too, little star. Daddy just couldn't stand the thought of you all alone without anyone here. He thought since Sunshine is practically part of the family, we needed to find a way to get her here."

"There's my little star," Dad called from across the barn. He chuckled as I ran to him. He spun me around and hugged me close.

I held tight to Dad's hand. "Thank you, Daddy. I'm so happy you found a way to bring Sunshine to me."

"I have some extra clothes for you," Mom said, holding up a bag. "And I brought your sleeping bag because Maria said you might camp under the stars. Why don't you show us your cabin?"

Lisa popped her head around the door of the barn. "Starley, I'm sorry to break up your reunion, but Maria needs you in the ring."

Megan gave me a quick hug. "I'll do it, Mom. You can watch Starley ride."

Dad held Sunshine while I mounted. They trailed alongside as I walked her back to the arena.

Maria trotted her horse to the gate. "Thanks so much, Mr. and Mrs. Robinson. Please don't take this wrong, but I don't allow parents to watch me train. It makes the kids skittish."

Mom frowned, but Dad just laughed. "I get it," he said, putting his arm around Mom's shoulder. "We'll get out of your hair."

Maria waited until they'd walked away before she resumed the lesson. She didn't insist I take the crop. We walked the course, then trotted over and over—getting the horses used to our commands.

"Great work, kids," Maria said. "It's time to take care of your horses." She caught my eye and winked.

I leaned over and patted Sunshine's neck. My heart was so light, it felt like it might float away.

Liko held Pilikia back so Sunshine and I could follow Heidi. "Nice horse," he said.

I wanted to tell him he handled Pilikia way better than I did. I wanted to thank him. But none of it came out. So instead, I smiled.

"The famous Sunshine," Heidi said, handing me

a brush when I dismounted. "I see why you love her so much."

"She's pretty," Kristina said grudgingly. "Not as pretty as my Butterscotch, but she has a nice gait."

Pumai handed me a pick. "Can you show me how you get her to take those turns so fast?"

I nodded. I felt like I did when Megan let me tag along with her and her friends. I lifted Sunshine's hoof and picked mud out of her shoe. I peeked through her legs at Heidi brushing Mango. She smiled at me, and I smiled back.

Sunshine looked back at me with her usual patience and love.

"I love you, too," I whispered.

Chapter 10
New Friends

After dinner, the other girls went back to the cabin, and I checked in on Sunshine. “Brought you something, girl,” I said, holding out my palm.

Sunshine snuffled the edge of my fingers before finally taking the sugar cube. Her ears faced forward, and I could tell she was happy to be here. I smoothed her mane. “I’ll see you tomorrow.”

Sunshine pushed her nose against me in the same way she always did at home. I hugged her tight, happiness filling me along with the yummy banana pudding from dinner.

As I turned around to leave, I was surprised to see Liko standing outside the barn door. "We're not supposed to go to the stables at night," he said.

"Oh, I didn't know," I said with a shrug.

He pulled out an apple from behind his back and grinned. "Looks like we had the same idea."

I smiled. "Yeah. See you tomorrow."

He nodded as he walked past, toward Pilikia. "Not if I see you first."

I appreciated that the darkness hid my flaming red cheeks. I waited for a second before I made a beeline for my cabin. I pulled off my boots and lined them up with the rest of the shoes by the front door. I was halfway down the hall when a scream came from the direction of the bathroom.

Heidi ran out with a towel wrapped around her.

"I saw the biggest cockroach inside the bathroom," she gasped. "I'm not going back in there until it's dead."

"Don't be a baby," Pumai said with a wrinkled nose. "Just smack it with a shoe."

"Ew," Kristina said. "Call the janitor."

"There's no janitor," Pumai said. "This is horse *camp*. We're supposed to rough it. Just whack it with your slipper."

I left them arguing and walked cautiously into the bathroom. A cockroach crawled up the side of the shower. I took off one of my rubber slippers and walked slowly toward it. "I'm sorry," I whispered. "But I promise to make it quick."

The cockroach stopped. Its antennae waggled in my direction. I started imagining its family, with little baby cockroaches at home that might miss him. I let my slipper drop to the floor.

"Looks like I'm going to have to make a bug trap," I said. "Don't worry, I'm a pro at this."

I ripped the top off a tissue box and grabbed a paper cup. I moved fast and slid the cup down the wall while slipping the cardboard underneath it. I flipped the cup over. The cardboard kept the cockroach trapped inside until I could let him go.

The lights from the cabin shone on the bushes on the opposite side of the barn. I turned the cockroach loose. "Go back to your babies," I whispered, hoping his home wasn't back inside the cabin.

"What was in the cup?" Evan asked. He and Greg were tossing a football back and forth, the silver glow of the moon their only light.

"A cockroach," I said and braced myself to be teased.

"Cool," Greg said. "Want to play?"

I took a quick look back at the cabin. "Maybe for

just a minute."

Greg threw the ball to me. Not too fast, but not taking it easy on me, either. I caught it and threw a spiral to Evan. "Nice arm," he said.

I caught it a few more times before I turned to go back inside. "Good night," Greg called.

"Night," I said, turning so they wouldn't see my smile. It finally felt like I was starting to fit in.

A thin layer of sweat beaded across my upper lip as I ran inside. "It's gone," I announced to the girls. They stopped in the middle of their argument about who should kill the cockroach. "I took care of it."

"*You* took care of it?" Kristina asked, with one eyebrow arched.

Pumai grinned. "For real? I knew behind all that quiet-girl stuff hid a warrior!"

"My hero," Heidi said, jumping up and hugging me. "Did you flush it?"

I shrugged.

"But it's really gone?" Heidi quickly glanced back at the bathroom like she expected to see the cockroach come flying out at her.

I nodded. "Yes."

Kristina laughed. "You're just full of surprises. Well, this calls for a celebration." She walked to her top drawer and pulled out a bag of candy. "You get first choice."

I picked a giant chocolate bar. The girls each took one.

Pumai motioned to us. "Come, let's play a game." She sat on the floor next to her bed and patted the space next to her. "Sit here, Starley."

I dropped to the floor. Kristina sat opposite me, and Heidi moved next to her. Pumai dealt the cards. "Let's start easy. Everyone know how to play Go Fish?"

I took a bite of my candy bar and watched as each girl looked at her cards. I liked Heidi and maybe Pumai. I wasn't so sure about Kristina. But Tutu always said if you gave people a chance, they might surprise you.

Chapter 11
The Fall of a Hero

Heidi handed me a horse blanket. It was cold inside the barn, so we saddled our horses quickly. Pumai finished first, with a triumphant fist pump in the air. "Beat that time," she said with a grin.

I finished next and led Sunshine out of the barn.

"We're going on a trail ride this morning," Liko called out to us. He was riding Pilikia.

"Maria said we deserved a break," Greg said as he walked his horse in circles.

Pumai pulled herself up into the saddle and waited for me. Once we were all ready, one of the ranch hands guided us along a trail leading up the mountain. Sunshine and I followed Kristina and her horse, Butterscotch. Heidi and Mango were behind us. The trees were thick as a curtain, until they finally thinned out and the valley stretched out below us in different shades of green.

When we reached a small stream, water splashed the bottom of my jeans as we crossed it. Finally, we reached an open field. "I challenge Starley to a race!" Evan shouted. Before I could reply, he'd taken off in a gallop. Without another second to lose, I urged Sunshine to follow.

The others raced behind us. I laughed as the wind whipped my hair until it stood up straight. I inched into the lead and stopped at the edge of the field.

Greg laughed. "Looks like you don't need the crop after all," he said with a friendly smile.

Kristina's eyes sparkled. I could tell she loved to ride as much as I did. At least we had that in common. "Race you back," she said to no one in particular.

We all took up the challenge. This wasn't winning, but it sure was fun.

The whole way back we told stories. Where Evan left off, Greg would continue, and then Heidi. Each of us took a turn. When it was mine, I told the story of my tutu learning to ride. How she came from a long line of paniolos, and how I wanted to be just like her.

During lunch, I looked around at the other campers. We teased one another and laughed. I finally felt like I belonged here.

"It's time," Maria said. She held out the crop. "I know you don't want to, but I promise Sunshine won't be hurt. If you're serious about being a champion, then you need to do the necessary work. And that includes learning to motivate your horse beyond what she normally gives you."

I took the crop automatically. I looked at it and then at my friends. The last week I'd learned so much, and I finally felt like a part of this group. They all looked at me like they expected me to do whatever Maria asked. They'd all done it.

My thoughts tumbled around in my head.

Can I use it? Do I really need to do this to be a champion? Is this the only way to keep Sunshine?

"Now, when you take Sunshine through the course, I want you to tap her flank gently. You're not trying to hurt her. You just want to grab her attention and motivate her to go faster—to give you all she has." Maria's smile was gentle. "It's a tool, just like the bridle or the bit. Those aren't natural to a horse, but we use them, right?"

I nodded. It was true. So why did every part of me want to throw the crop as far away from me as I could?

"You've already improved so much, Starley. I'm so impressed with you," Maria said. "You need to trust me. Can you do that? Can you trust me?"

I nodded again. I thought about all the things I'd learned so far. Riding a horse was a privilege. Maria said so. We needed to treat them with respect. *But I already treat Sunshine with respect. How will she ever trust me if I hurt her?*

I clucked my tongue and urged Sunshine into a trot. We picked up speed as we rounded the first barrel. I held the crop close.

"Now, Starley," Maria called. "Give her a tap."

The crop felt like it weighed more than it did a few seconds ago. I held it out. We rounded the next corner. I asked Sunshine to go faster with my words and a gentle squeeze of my legs, but not with the crop. I couldn't. I let it slip out of my fingers and drop to the ground. I held the reins straight out in front of me and tapped my heels against her side.

Sunshine and I raced around the barrels. I could tell we were going faster than we had ever gone before. Wind hit my face and made my eyes water. We finished, and I slowed Sunshine to a trot.

I pulled to a stop in front of Maria. I couldn't keep the grin from stealing across my face. "See how fast she ran? I told you I didn't need it!"

Maria stared at me with her red lips flattened in a straight line. "Get off your horse and meet me in my office," she growled. Before I could say anything in reply, she turned on her heels and stomped off.

I looked at Heidi. Her eyes were wide. Kristina frowned, and Pumai shook her head.

Liko ran to where I'd dropped the crop and picked it up. He turned to me and gave a little half smile. "It was nice knowing you, haole girl."

"Maybe she won't get kicked out," Heidi said hopefully.

"She's out," Evan said.

Greg nodded, but he didn't look happy. "Yep."

"You were kind of growing on me," Kristina said with a shrug. "Sorry, Starley."

My stomach felt like I'd swallowed a rock. "You think she's kicking me out? Just because I didn't use the crop?"

"Because you didn't listen to her," Pumai corrected.

I swung my leg out of the saddle and slid off Sunshine. I looked at each of their faces. "Really?" I asked, not wanting to believe this was the end.

Heidi rushed to my side and hugged me. "You were so brave."

I took Sunshine's reins and led her to the barn. Lisa came out of the tack room. "I'll take her. Maria wants to talk to you."

Sunshine butted my shoulder softly. I gave her a quick hug. "I could never have done it," I whispered against her neck. "I'm sorry I even thought about it."

My boots tapped against the wood floor. Each step echoed in my ears until I stood in front of Maria.

"I saw so much potential in you, Starley." Maria sat on the edge of her desk and frowned at me. "You let me down. You let yourself down. And you let Sunshine down. If an animal doesn't know who's in charge, then they don't feel safe. How will she ever truly trust you? I'm sorry it's come to this, but I've called your parents. They should be here in the next hour and a half. You have that time to pack and say goodbye to the other campers."

My mouth opened, but my voice froze. All I could do was nod. I had so many things I wanted to say, but the words stayed locked up tight inside of me. I turned around and made my way to my dorm. I packed everything and looked around the small cabin. Memories of card games and scary stories filled the room. Even the small bunk bed had finally started to feel like mine.

Heidi slammed the door open, and the girls rushed to my side. "I can't believe you're really going! We weren't supposed to say goodbye for another week," Heidi wailed.

Pumai patted my shoulder. "This stinks."

Kristina made her way to her dresser and pulled out her bag of candy. She held it out to me. "You'll need this more than I will."

I took the bag. “Thank you.” I looked at each of them. “I’m going to miss you guys.”

Heidi hooked her arm in mine and walked with me. Kristina and Pumai trailed behind. The boys were waiting at the barn.

Liko bumped his fist lightly against mine. “You’re a good rider. I hope we compete against each other one day.”

I smiled. “Me too.”

Greg jerked his chin up. “See you.”

Evan frowned. “This is messed up.”

I moved to the steps and sat down. I couldn’t believe this was really happening. I didn’t even get past phase one of my plan. How would I win the rodeo now? And if I didn’t win, then how would I buy Sunshine?

Chapter 12
Home Again

Mom and Dad were quiet as they helped load Sunshine into the trailer. Maria was nowhere to be seen. Lisa was the one who handed Mom the paperwork. "Here is the waiver Mr. Griffin, the owner, signed. You can tell him we'll cancel the insurance."

"The owner?" Heidi asked, her face a mask of confusion. "I thought Sunshine was yours."

I tried to explain. "I meant to tell you—"

Kristina sniffed and rolled her eyes. "Figures."

"We need to hit the road, hon," Mom said, putting her arm around my shoulders and leading me to the car.

I waved. My new friends stood in a straggly line and watched me go. My heart hurt as we drove down the long driveway and turned onto the road leading home.

"We're here if you want to talk about it," Dad said, meeting my eyes in the rearview mirror.

Mom turned and held out her hand. "Maria said you refused to listen to her. That's just not like you, Starley."

I could always talk to my parents. My voice never froze with them. But this time was different. This time I wasn't sure if they would take my side.

I looked out the window and kept quiet. Mom turned back around with a sigh. "We can wait until we get home to talk about this."

My mind raced. I had been so sure that Maria could teach me to be the best. *If I still enter the rodeo, am I good enough to win?*

The trees and ocean we drove by were the same. Our driveway and house looked the same, too. But the drive home felt longer than I remembered. Tutu greeted me with open arms. She didn't ask what had happened. "I'll go with you to take Sunshine back to the old coot."

We led Sunshine back through the pasture. Tutu didn't say anything even when Mr. Griffin greeted us at the barn.

"I thought you had her until next week," he boomed, his mustache twitching as he spoke. "Get tired of her, did you?"

"No! I could never get tired of her," I said.

"Then what's the story, girly?" He smiled and

waited with his arms folded across his chest.

I waited for my words to freeze like they always did. But when I opened my mouth, it all poured out. I could tell Tutu was as surprised as I was.

Mr. Griffin tugged at his mustache while he listened. When I was done, he didn't say anything at first. He looked past me and toward the barn. "Come back tomorrow, young lady. I have an idea."

"What time?" Tutu asked, as if she'd expected this.

"Early morning," he answered, with a wave of his hand.

"We will be here." Tutu grabbed my hand, and we headed away from the barn and down the driveway.

"Do you think he's going to tell me I can't sponsor Sunshine anymore?" I swallowed hard and blinked the tears away.

"I do not," she said with a quick shake of her head. "He would never find anyone who cares as much as you do, and he knows it. Did you know Sunshine belonged to Mr. Griffin's wife? She rode every morning, right up until the day she died."

"She did?" I asked, my head spinning. I didn't know that. And now I had one more thing to worry about. *What if Mr. Griffin won't sell Sunshine to me even if I do have the money?*

"His wife loved that horse. It's why he hasn't sold her. So there's nothing to worry about. As long as you love Sunshine and treat her right, he will continue to let you sponsor her."

"But what if I want more?" I asked.

Tutu held my hand as we walked up the steep part of the driveway. "Then you need to ask yourself why you want more. Especially when you already have so much."

I thought about that while I unpacked. I ate the sandwich Mom made me and helped with the dishes. And the whole time I rolled the words Tutu had said around and around in my mind. By the end of the day, I still didn't understand them.

Chapter 13
Someone New

The next morning, I shot out of bed, pulled on my riding jeans, and rushed to the kitchen. Mom held up a hand. "Whoa, there, cowgirl. Breakfast first, then you can go see Sunshine."

I grabbed a granola bar. "I have to hurry, Mom. Mr. Griffin said I needed to come over this morning."

"Okay, okay." She smiled in the way she always did when I talked about horses and Sunshine. Like she understood completely. "Tell Mr. Griffin I'm still making him his favorite cookies this week. I haven't forgotten."

"Yes, Mom," I called over my shoulder as I ran across the pasture.

Mr. Griffin wasn't outside the barn. I slowed, listening for his gravelly voice. Now that I knew about his wife, he seemed less scary. I peeked inside and caught sight of his white hair and stooped shoulders. He was talking to someone in one of the stalls.

The heels of my boots echoed in the large barn. He looked my way and waved his arm. "There you are, young lady. I was just telling Bethany about you. Come here, come here. Don't be shy."

He stepped away from the stall. A tall woman leaned out and looked me up and down. Her hair was streaked with gray and pulled back in a long braid. Faint wrinkles spread across her face and deepened when she smiled at me.

"This is Bethany Keohokapu," he said. "She helps me train some of my more difficult horses. I think she might be able to help you."

Bethany walked toward me with her hand held out. She took mine and held on tight. "Nice to meet you, Starley. Mr. Griffin says you would like to get ready for a rodeo. Is that right?"

I nodded and looked at Mr. Griffin. I still needed to ask him about riding Sunshine in the Hilo rodeo.

Mr. Griffin rocked back on his heels and smiled like he could read my mind. "I'm planning on shipping a couple of my horses over to the Big Island to compete. I have a good mind to include Sunshine. If you ride her, will you promise to win?"

"I would try!" I smiled so hard my cheeks hurt.

"With Bethany training you, there won't be anything you can't do," Mr. Griffin said. "I'll leave you to it. Come see me about the other thing later, Beth. We'll talk more then."

Bethany nodded. "Of course, Jed." She waited until we were alone and then turned to me with a raised brow. "I hear you trained briefly with Maria?"

"Yes," I said softly.

"I know her. She actually trained with me." It seemed like Bethany was waiting for her words to sink in. She smiled gently and continued, "Before we start, I think we should establish some rules. How does that sound?"

I cleared my throat. "Good."

"Good," Bethany repeated. "I expect, from what Mr. Griffin told me, you might want to know what I think about using crops and whips?"

"Will I have to use one?" I asked, my voice barely over a whisper.

Bethany tilted her head. "Would it bother you if

I said you would?"

My throat felt tight, like my words might freeze again. "Yes. But I know it's silly to feel that way. I know it's just a tool, like a bit or a bridle. I just . . . I can't."

"That's true. It *is* a tool," Bethany said calmly. "And I'm not one to dismiss something that may be needed with certain horses. But Sunshine isn't one of those horses. If we can train a horse with love and understanding, then that's the best way. How does that sound?"

It sounded better than I could have hoped. I wanted to thank her and tell her how much I looked forward to learning from her. But all I could do was grin.

She motioned for me to follow her. "Let's go get that horse of yours."

"She's Mr. Griffin's horse," I corrected. "She

doesn't belong to me."

"Mr. Griffin may own her, but she's *your* horse, yeah?" Bethany stopped at Sunshine's stall.

Sunshine greeted me with a low whinny. I scratched the soft spot on her muzzle. "Hey, girl. You must be tired after that long drive yesterday. Are you happy to be home?"

Bethany held her hand out for Sunshine to smell. "Tomorrow we'll meet here at six-thirty in the morning, sharp. I'll help train you, yeah? Does that sound good to you?"

"Yes, Mrs. Keohokapu."

"Call me Bethany. Mrs. Keohokapu is my mother-in-law." Bethany scrunched her nose and grinned.

"Yes, Bethany," I said with a smile of my own.

"And Starley," Bethany said. "I believe in listening to your horse and your heart. I never want you to do anything that your heart doesn't agree with. Okay?"

I nodded.

"If you do that, then you are already a winner." She smiled and held out her fist. I bumped it with mine. I thought about her words as we walked toward Mr. Griffin's porch. How could I be a winner without actually winning?

Chapter 14
Aloha KaKahiaKa

The early-morning sun painted the sky pink and orange. I trudged through the pasture on my way to Mr. Griffin's for my first lesson with Bethany. The grass smelled like the rain from last night. I closed the gate behind me. Sunshine whinnied and ran to the edge of the arena. Her ears pointed forward as she watched me approach.

Bethany sat on the railing next to her. "Aloha kakahiaka," she called to me. "Sunshine and I are getting better acquainted. She says she loves sugar cubes more than anything."

I giggled. "She does like sugar cubes."

"And so do I," she said, popping a sugar cube into her mouth. "Are you ready to get started?"

I held out my hand and let Sunshine nuzzle me. "Yes, Mrs. Keoho—Bethany."

"After you warm up, I'd like you to take Sunshine through her laterals. Then we can walk the course together."

I looked at the barrels placed around the arena. I couldn't believe it was only yesterday that I'd run a different course. "What if I'm not ready?" I asked.

"Then we'll get you ready." Bethany hopped down and untied the large gray gelding tied to the post. "This is Maverick. He's *my* Sunshine."

"He's beautiful," I said. I watched how she took Maverick through the course in a canter that almost looked like they were in slow motion.

"Now, it's your turn," she said.

I walked Sunshine around the barrels several times. Then I nudged her into a trot. Finally, we ran the barrels at full speed.

"Good job!" Bethany called. "Now walk her again."

Sunshine tossed her head like she still wanted to run. "No, girl. That's enough for now."

I leaned closer to Sunshine's neck and told her what a good girl she was.

"Good job, Starley." Bethany smiled briefly. "I have a few things I'd like you to work on. We can talk while you groom Sunshine."

I brushed Sunshine and watched Bethany while she picked stones and debris out of her horse's hooves. I felt like I might explode while I waited to hear what she thought I needed to work on. Would she tell me I was hopeless?

"So . . . ," Bethany started. "I'd like to see you listen to your instincts more. I can see you hesitating before you give Sunshine a command. She'll sense that, and it will confuse her. You have to be confident so she can have confidence in you."

I opened my mouth to tell her I *was* confident, but my words froze like they always did. Bethany looked at me as if she were waiting for me to respond. I nodded like I understood what she'd said, even though I didn't.

"That's what I'm talking about," Bethany said with a frown. "You obviously disagree with me, and yet you nod as if you don't. I want honesty. Can you give that to me?"

"I just don't understand what you want from me," I said, my voice louder than I'd planned. I snapped my mouth shut and felt my face turn pink.

Now she'd yell at me for sure. Tell me she couldn't train me.

But Bethany didn't yell. One side of her mouth lifted in a lopsided smile. "That's what I want! I want you to tell me what you're feeling. That's the only way this is going to work. Horses are extremely sensitive to our emotions. We need to understand our own feelings so we don't confuse them, yeah?"

I nodded. "But how do I do that?"

"Start with telling me how you felt at the camp. Did you enjoy learning from Maria?" Bethany placed her horse's hoof down and hung up the pick.

I thought about it. "I think so. Most of the time. But when we didn't do what Maria said, she would yell. I didn't like that."

Bethany handed me a curry comb. "There's no need to worry about any yelling here with me. I don't think it helps. What else? Good or bad."

"I didn't like how she tried to make me use the crop," I said. "I know you don't think Sunshine needs it. But I don't think we should use them on *any* horses. I think it's mean."

Bethany ran a hand over her braid as she thought about what I'd said. I liked how she didn't shrug off my opinions just because I was a kid.

"Well, I'm not going to lie," she said carefully. "I *have* used crops and whips, and even spurs, in training a horse. Some needed the motivation. But I understand why you think it's cruel. You're not alone. There are plenty of people who think there are other ways to get a horse to listen to you. I agree, for the most part. Don't worry that I'll ever try to make you do anything you feel uncomfortable about. Okay?"

It felt like a gigantic boulder had rolled off my shoulders. I smiled and nodded. "Thank you."

"I have something else I'd like to ask you. I run a small working ranch not far from here. Would you like to make some extra money working there? I can talk to Mr. Griffin about bringing Sunshine over, if it's something you'd be interested in."

"Yes!" I blurted out.

She laughed. "Don't you want to ask how much I'd pay you?"

I felt my face get pink. "I guess?"

She laughed again. "Ask your parents, and I'll ask Mr. Griffin. We'll talk more tomorrow."

"Okay!" I ran home full of energy. It really was a good morning. I'd always wanted to work on a ranch, just like a real paniolo!

Chapter 15

Paniolo

"It's too early in the morning for you to be this happy," Megan said grouchily. She pulled out a box of cereal and poured the last of it into a bowl. "Mom said I had to be nice to you because you're sad. You don't look sad to me."

I danced around the kitchen. "My new trainer, Bethany, is awesome! And she offered me a job being a paniolo at her ranch."

"Are you dropping the rodeo idea?" Megan asked

between bites of cereal.

Not even Megan slurping the milk off her spoon bugged me like it usually did. “I can do both.”

One of Megan’s eyebrows waggled. “What happened at that camp, anyway? Mom said you’re not talking about it.”

I shrugged. I thought about telling her. I even pictured how she’d react, but the words stayed put. “It’s nothing.”

Megan gave me a look that said I wasn’t fooling her. “Fine. Don’t tell me. Just don’t ask for any of my secrets.”

I started to protest when I realized she would never tell me any of her secrets, anyway. “Nice try,” I said instead.

She laughed. “You’re growing up, Star. It used to be so easy to trick you.”

Mom gave me her permission to work at Bethany's ranch after she'd talked to Mr. Griffin. "She's a really well-respected trainer," Mom told Dad. "And she owns a small cattle ranch that's pretty profitable. I guess she only trains horses for a select few."

"And she's training our Starley?" Dad looked over at me and made one of his silly faces.

"As a favor to Jed Griffin," Mom said. "They're old friends. And you know how fond he is of Starley."

Mr. Griffin is fond of me? I thought he didn't like me. I frowned. Sometimes it felt like I was getting everything wrong. People I thought would help me didn't, and those I thought were against me were actually on my side.

"Well, I suppose working with her would be good for Starley," Dad said.

I danced in place, unable to hold in my happiness any longer. Dad laughed. Mom came over and gave me one of her biggest hugs.

"And just so you know, Tutu told us about what happened at camp. I've a good mind to call up that Maria woman. She acted disgracefully." Mom squeezed me tighter. "I'm so proud of you. Standing up for what you believe in is exactly the right thing to have done."

Dad ruffled my hair. "That's our little star."

I hugged Mom back. I was glad they were proud of me. But a small part of me felt like I didn't deserve it. I'd wanted to fit in so bad that I almost did something that I didn't believe in. Bethany told me I needed to trust in my horse and my heart. From now on, that was exactly what I would do.

I thought about my plan.

Phase one: Become the best rodeo rider.

I couldn't ask for a better trainer than Bethany. And working on her ranch and getting paid to do what I loved would put me that much closer to my dream.

Phase two: Compete in the Hilo rodeo.

Mr. Griffin had already agreed to let me enter the competition with Sunshine. So I just needed to find a way to get myself there.

Phase three: Buy Sunshine.

For the first time, my dream felt real—like it might actually happen. All I needed to do was reach out and grab it.

Chapter 16
Special

Mom walked with me to the barn at Bethany's ranch. They talked for a minute while I looked around. The barn was brand-new but smaller than Mr. Griffin's. Mom kissed me goodbye, and I followed Bethany inside. The barn was dark and smelled like a mixture of hay and fly spray.

"These are my ranch hands, Manny and Leo." Bethany looped her arm around my shoulder. "And this is Starley."

They nodded to me. I could see they were wondering why I was there.

"You're with me, Starley," Bethany said. "I have to ride to the end of the fence line on the east side. Our cows are getting out somewhere, and we need to find the hole in the fence and fix it. Sound good?"

I nodded eagerly. The weather today felt like the bathroom after a hot shower. My shirt was already wet with sweat. I didn't care because I was getting to be a true paniolo. I tugged my cowboy hat down lower. Sunshine danced. I could tell she was eager to run. I was, too.

Bethany cantered over the pasture and down a hill. The breeze felt good on my face. Sunshine kept up with Maverick as he went faster and faster. I held the horn with one hand and my reins in the other. I loved how it felt like we were flying. I laughed with the joy of it.

I glanced at Bethany, but she wasn't laughing. Her face looked serious, like she was concentrating on something important. Maybe a real paniolo didn't laugh when they were working.

We slowed as the fence came into view. Bethany pointed at a hole near a fallen tree. "Here's the problem." She hopped down and took out clippers from her saddlebag. She showed me how to fix the wire, patiently explaining things more than once until I got the hang of it.

"You're a natural," she said with a smile.

"It's fun!"

Bethany put both hands on her hips and looked out over her land. "This is the best job in the world," she stated. "I pinch myself every day. I could be working at my father's law firm—stuck in an office all day long."

I looked down at the valley below us. The dark

green reminded me of my tutu's jade earrings. "My dad does taxes," I said. "His office is really ugly."

"Nothing wrong with that," Bethany said, handing me another piece of wire. "If that's what you want."

We worked in silence until we were done. I liked how Bethany didn't need to talk all the time. I liked how the birds and the chickens were all the noise we needed.

The sun was setting when we rode back to her homestead. "Good work, Starley," she said. We dismounted and led our horses to the water trough. "Do you think you'd like to work again tomorrow?"

I nodded eagerly. "Yes, please."

"I'll call your mom and run it past her. If she says yes, you can leave Sunshine here. It'll be easier."

Manny helped me get the saddle off Sunshine. He didn't say much, but he was gentle with the horses. Sunshine nuzzled his shoulder, and he patted her fondly.

Leo handed Bethany a stack of papers, and they discussed something about the cattle. While Bethany called my mom, he looked over at me. "Hey," he said. "Beth says you were at that horse camp Maria runs?"

I nodded, trying to meet his gaze and not turn pink. I hated how talking to new people was always so hard.

"My nephew, Liko, is there now. He'll be here next week when he's pau with the camp."

I remembered Liko talking about his uncle being a paniolo. "You're the one who won the bull-riding event at the Hilo rodeo last year!"

He grinned, his dark eyes glinting with humor. "My reputation precedes me."

"Liko talked about you all the time," I said. "I

want to compete this year. Bethany's training me."

"Can't get any better than that," Leo said. "She doesn't take on new people anymore. You must be special."

His words made me feel like when I raced with Sunshine—free and full of joy. Maybe I wasn't a failure if Bethany thought I was special.

Chapter 17

Don't Take My Sunshine Away

Mr. Griffin visited Bethany's ranch the next day. His mustache drooped like he'd forgotten to brush it. "Hey, girly," he said to me.

I led Sunshine out of the barn and put her in the pasture. She sniffed my shoulder delicately before she turned and trotted to the middle. "Hey, Mr. Griffin! Bethany is in her office. I can get her if you'd like."

He waved a hand. "No, no. You're the person I

was hoping to speak with."

My stomach tightened like it does before I'm about to compete. "Oh, yeah?"

"I've been thinking about Sunshine lately. You know she was my late wife's horse?"

I nodded. Mr. Griffin looked straight at me, and his eyes seemed so sad. I wanted to make him feel better. "She's the best horse," I said. "Truly."

He cleared his throat and looked out at where Sunshine grazed. "Yes, she is."

I struggled with what to say next. I wondered if now was a good time to ask him if I could buy her. But something in his expression stopped me.

"I've been thinking a lot about my wife lately," Mr. Griffin said, a wobble in his voice. "And I need to honor her memory more than I have. I've been contemplating what would happen to Sunshine if something were to happen to me. And . . ."

My heart jumped in my chest. Excitement flooded me. He was going to give Sunshine to me, I could feel it!

"I've decided to send Sunshine to my granddaughter. She lives in the mainland. I think that's what my Helen would have wanted." Mr. Griffin stared at Sunshine so he didn't see how his words hit me.

It felt like all the air in the world wouldn't be enough to keep my lungs going. "But . . . but . . ." I gasped as the words left my mouth. I wanted to tell him how much I loved Sunshine—how she meant more to me than almost anything. But my words froze inside my mouth like they always did.

"Don't you worry," Mr. Griffin said. "I think Bethany has a horse you can use. Maybe even sponsor. How does that sound?"

My whole body trembled. I nodded.

He patted the top of my head. "Good girl. Tell Bethany I'll call her later."

Panic filled me. I hopped the fence and ran to Sunshine. I needed to get her out of here. Fast. That way he couldn't take her away from me.

Sunshine and I made it halfway to the south pasture before Bethany caught up with me. "Hooey," she called out.

My face felt like it was hotter than the sun. I pulled back on the reins and slowed Sunshine to a walk. "How did you find me?"

"Leo saw you ride off after Mr. Griffin left." Bethany's mouth turned down sympathetically. "He told me what he wants to do with Sunshine. I'm guessing that's why you were riding out here?"

"I can't let him send her away." I could feel tears on my face, and I wiped them away impatiently. I didn't have time to cry.

"Did you tell Mr. Griffin how you feel?" Bethany asked. "I've always found him to be a reasonable man."

I shook my head. "It won't matter what I say. He's sad about his wife."

Bethany waved an arm. "What were you planning on doing with Sunshine out here? Keep her hidden until the rodeo?"

I shrugged sheepishly. "I didn't really think it through. I just wanted to hide her."

"Not a great plan." She twisted in her seat and hooked a thumb in the direction of the ranch. "Why don't we head back? I bet you can think of a better one on the way."

We walked the horses slowly. "I love Sunshine," I said. "I don't want any horse. I want her. But when Mr. Griffin asked me what I thought, I froze. I let him think I was okay with Sunshine being sent away."

"Do you think it might have made a difference to Mr. Griffin if you told him how you felt?" Bethany asked.

"Maybe? He loves Sunshine because his wife loved her." I thought about Mr. Griffin's face when he looked at Sunshine—how there was sadness but also a softness that reminded me of how I felt when I looked at her. "If he truly loves Sunshine, then he wants what's best for her."

Bethany smiled at me. "Are you what's best for her?"

"I know what treats she loves," I said. "And how she doesn't like to be brushed too hard. I know how smart she is. I know no one will ever love her as much as I do."

Bethany nodded. "Well, I'm convinced."

"But . . . sometimes I have a hard time saying how I feel. I can't get the words out."

“Maybe you can write it down and practice saying it out loud. Like a script,” Bethany suggested.

We rode in silence while I thought about her idea. It reminded me of how I would sometimes write notes to Mom or Dad when I really wanted to get all of my thoughts out clearly. “What if I wrote him a letter?” I asked hopefully. “Do you think that would work?”

“Like most things, you never know until you try,” Bethany said.

Chapter 18

The Letter

Later that night, I stared at the blank piece of paper I'd gotten from Mom. I'd decided to write Mr. Griffin a letter. That way I could make my arguments without being afraid I'd mess it up somehow. My voice couldn't freeze in a letter.

Megan plopped down on the end of my bed. "How's it going? Need any help with what to say?"

"I'm okay," I said. "I just hope it works."

Megan tapped her finger on my ankle. "Tutu's

ready to go to battle for you. You know you have all of us on your side, yeah?"

I nodded. "I know. Thanks."

~

The next day my stomach hurt as I handed the letter over to Mr. Griffin.

"What's this?" he asked, both of his bushy eyebrows shooting up.

I tangled my fingers together to keep them from trembling. "A letter. For you," I said softly.

He nodded and motioned for me to follow him onto the porch, where he sat with a huge sigh. I perched on the rocker next to him, keeping my legs straight so the chair stayed still.

It didn't take long until he finished. He set the paper down gently against his knees and looked at me. "Well, why didn't you say all of this yesterday?"

I shrugged, my face burning. "I wanted to."

He stared at me and finally nodded. "I bet you didn't know that my dear Helen was very shy. She surely did love to write, though. That woman wrote me many a letter. I treasured each one." He looked across the porch and toward the pasture. "She loved it here, and she loved her horses."

I stayed silent. I didn't want to interrupt his memories.

"I tell you what," he said finally. "I'll take you up on your offer, young lady. If you want to buy my wife's horse, then I would be heartless not to allow it. Especially given how much you seem to love Sunshine. But, first and foremost, I'm a businessman, so you will have to pay me what she's worth. Can you do that?"

I felt as if I might float away. I grinned so hard my face hurt. "Yes! Thank you, Mr. Griffin." My smile slipped. What if he wanted more than the prize money? "How much *is* she worth, sir?"

"I could sell her for up to seven thousand dollars. But for you . . ." He paused and squinted at me as if he were measuring how tall I was. "Let's say five thousand dollars. How does that sound?"

I let out a relieved sigh. "It sounds great!"

Now I just had to win the rodeo.

Chapter 19
Reunion

Bethany trained me every day after the morning chores. She changed up the routine so Sunshine and I would be ready for anything. I'd just finished cooling Sunshine down with a brisk walk when I heard a familiar voice.

"Hey, Starley! I didn't know you worked here." Liko waved from behind the arena fence.

I nudged Sunshine in his direction and flashed a cautious smile. I couldn't forget how I'd left the camp. I wondered what he thought of me.

"Your uncle Leo said you'd be here this week," I said, feeling my face get pink like always. "Bethany's training me for the Hilo rodeo."

"I'm competing, too!" He grinned and opened the gate for me. "Heidi will be there. I'm not sure about everyone else."

Liko motioned toward Sunshine. "Are you bringing her? I'm riding one of my cousin's horses."

"Yep." I couldn't think of what else to say so I led Sunshine past him.

He fell in step with me. "Hey, um, I wanted to let you know I told my parents how Maria treated you. They agreed that I shouldn't go there next year. It wasn't right—that she tried to make you do something you weren't cool with."

I stopped and looked at him with wide eyes. "Really? That's so nice of you."

He looked at the ground and kicked the dirt with his scuffed-up boots. "I can be nice."

"Don't worry," I said with a teasing smile. "I won't tell anyone."

He laughed. "Thanks."

"Liko, I was wondering where you went," Leo said from inside the barn. "There's plenty to do, nephew. Hurry, eh?"

"Yes, Unko," Liko said quickly. He lifted his chin. "Laters, Starley."

The next couple of weeks fell into a familiar pattern. Bethany and I got to the point where Sunshine moved exactly when I wanted her to—sometimes a second before I even gave a command.

"You're going to dominate," Liko said after our end-of-the-day run-through. "No way anyone else will be able to touch that time."

I leaned down and rubbed Sunshine's sweaty neck. "I hope so. I don't know what I'll do if we don't."

Liko ran a hand across his spiky hair. "When Heidi gets here, we can make a plan. Make sure you win."

I rolled my eyes. I could imagine the kind of plan he'd dream up. It would probably include eating my weight in taro chips and trying to ride the grumpy bull out in the left pasture. "The only plan I need is to do my best."

"Relax!" He held up his hands. "I just meant we need to make sure you don't get all nervous and blow it."

I opened my mouth to argue, but he was right. Sometimes my nerves did get in the way of doing my best. I bit my lip and looked at the old rusty clock ticking on the wall. Heidi should be here any minute. "I guess," I said. Before I could say anything else, a car door slammed.

"That's probably her," Liko said, smoothing the sides of his hair.

I quickly tied Sunshine to a post and darted toward the front of the barn. Liko didn't run, but when I glanced back, he was definitely walking faster.

"Heidi!" I called.

"Starley!" Heidi ran straight to me with a huge grin. We clutched each other's arms and jumped up and down. "I missed you! My mom was getting legit mad at how much I was talking about you." Heidi wrapped her arm around my shoulder and waved at Liko.

"Hey." He nodded like it was no big deal she was here. "Long time no see."

Heidi shot him a huge smile. "Does that mean you missed me?"

Liko rolled his eyes, but one side of his mouth lifted like he was trying not to smile.

"I wanted to say something," I said, taking a deep breath.

Heidi tilted her head. "Shoot."

"I'm sorry for acting like I really owned Sunshine when I only sponsor her. It wasn't honest." I forced myself to hold her gaze and not look away.

"I hope you know that kind of stuff doesn't matter to me," Heidi said slowly.

"You all had your own horses, and Kristina already was making a big deal about the scholarship," I quickly explained. "And even though I don't own her, Sunshine and I belong to each other. That's why I *have* to win. If I don't, then I won't have enough money to buy her. I don't think it would take much for Mr. Griffin to change his mind and send Sunshine to his granddaughter in the mainland. Then I'd never see her, and I couldn't let that happen."

Heidi stared at me like I fascinated her. "That's the most I've ever heard you say at one time," she said with a small smile.

Liko snorted. "Don't worry. The more you spend time with her, the more she won't *stop* talking."

Chapter 20

Break a Saddle

"Remember that Tutu gets tired easily," Mom said, full of instructions. "No staying up late and keeping her awake. You can only go with Heidi or your other friends if Tutu says it's okay."

"Mom," I complained. "You've already gone over all this. Twice. I promise I'll listen to Tutu."

Dad pulled our suitcases out of the car and rolled them to the outdoor check-in for us. He gave Tutu a hug and then me. "Break a leg," he said as he kissed the top of my head.

"They only say that in show business, Dad," I said with a giggle.

"Okay, well then . . . break a saddle?" he teased.

"If we don't hurry, we'll miss our flight." Tutu waved her hand to me. "Hele on, keiki. Hurry, hurry."

Dad waved to the airport security guard who walked toward us. "Just dropping off. We're heading out!"

Mom and Dad drove off, and Tutu handed me one of her straw hats to carry. I used one hand to adjust my backpack and the other to carefully hold the brim.

Tutu sat down to put her shoes back on after we went through the security line. I was wearing my fancy rubber slippers—the ones with little flowers painted all over. Mom called them my airplane slippers.

"Have you heard from Bethany?" Tutu asked once she stood up.

I nodded. "She said Sunshine traveled really well. I miss her so much."

"Well, you'll see her soon enough. Right now, let's try not to miss our plane." Tutu hiked her purse up high on her shoulder and walked briskly toward our gate.

I glanced at the huge digital clock as I hurried to keep up. Our plane wasn't going to take off for three more hours. There was no way we were missing it. I bit my lip to keep from smiling. Mom said Tutu liked to be early to things because that's how she was raised.

"Thanks for taking me, Tutu," I said. "I'm not sure Mom would have let me go if it weren't for you."

She waved a hand like she was swatting a mosquito. "No need to thank me. I'm doing this for Sunshine as much as I'm doing it for you. That horse needs you."

I thought about that while we waited for our flight. *Does Sunshine need me as much as I need her?* I remembered how she always ran just a little faster when I rode her or how she seemed to listen to everything I said. I loved her more than anyone else ever could.

"But what if I don't win?" I whispered, finally saying out loud what worried me the most.

I didn't expect an answer. I didn't think Tutu had heard me until she reached out to squeeze my hand. "One thing at a time, keiki. Why worry about what you can't control?"

It was good advice. But no matter how hard I tried, I couldn't stop worrying.

Chapter 21
Hilo

Hilo was much smaller and less crowded than Honolulu. I watched the opening parade with Heidi and Liko. Pa'u riders with their beautiful, colorful gowns rode by. I loved how they decorated their horses with leis and flowers that represented each island. My island of Oahu was yellow for the 'ilima flower. Red ohia lehua flowers covered the rider representing the Big Island. Beautiful gowns and horses decorated in purple for Kaua'i, pink for

Maui, gray for Kahoʻolawe, orange for Lanai, green for Molokaʻi, and white for Niʻihau.

"This is boring," Liko muttered. "Who wants to watch a bunch of wahines with fancy dresses?"

"I do!" Heidi and I said at the same time. We laughed.

"Paʻu riders are very skilled," Tutu said from behind us.

Liko whipped around. "Sorry, Mrs. Robinson! I didn't mean any disrespect."

I elbowed Heidi, and she giggled.

Tutu put a hand on Liko's shoulder. "Maybe it will mean more to you if you understand the history behind it."

Liko nodded and looked down at his feet. "Yes, ma'am."

"I'm not a ma'am," Tutu said. "You can call me Aunty."

"Yes, Aunty," he said obediently.

"Wahines—or women—have been riding since the eighteen hundreds, just like the paniolos. They were extremely accomplished riders. They hiked up their fancy dresses and rode astride, like the men. To keep their beautiful dresses from getting dirty, they used a paʻu skirt to cover them. They are always the first in parades because they are part of our tradition."

"I never knew that," Liko said, looking at the riders with a new respect.

"My tutu used to be a paʻu rider," Heidi said. "We have her paʻu at home. Mom says I can have it when I'm older."

"That's very special," Tutu said, pulling the brim of her straw hat lower.

We watched the rest of the parade, and then it was time to head over to the stables. Bethany met me outside Sunshine's stall.

"How is she?" I asked. Sunshine stuck her neck out and sniffed at my hair. I scratched her favorite spot. "Hey, girl. I missed you."

"She's settling in very well," Bethany said. "I took her through her paces today and she's ready. I'd like you to get here tomorrow around six in the morning, and you can take a practice run before your first event."

"Can I just stay here with her for a while?" I asked Tutu.

Tutu nodded. "I'll go take a look around and see where I want to sit tomorrow. Meet me out by the bleachers when you're pau." She turned to Bethany. "If that's okay with you?"

Bethany smiled. "I'll stay with her and bring her out."

After Tutu left, I let myself into Sunshine's

stall. Bethany handed me a brush. “It always calms me to groom my horse before I compete. There’s something so soothing about it,” she said. “I will be outside if you need me.”

“Thanks.” I took the brush and stroked Sunshine’s coat slowly.

“I missed you so much, girl. Home doesn’t feel like home when you aren’t there.” Sunshine stood still, with both ears flicking forward and back as I talked to her. “We have to do our very best tomorrow. That way, we’ll never have to worry about being apart. You and I are a team, right?”

They say you can tell where a horse is looking by their ears. Hers faced me when I finished brushing her. “I know you’ll do your best, and I promise to do the same.”

I rubbed the area above her muzzle. It felt silky soft, and she lowered her head until it rested on the top of my shoulder. “I love you, Sunshine,” I whispered.

She nodded, her mane tickling my cheek. I hugged her neck. “I have something for you.” I pulled out a sugar cube, and she nibbled it out of my hand. “I’ll see you real soon, okay? Tomorrow will be here before you know it.”

She watched me with wise brown eyes that seemed to say she understood. I gave her one last pat and then went to find Bethany. I couldn’t wait to make Sunshine mine.

Chapter 22

"Hawai'i Pono'ī"

The next morning, the roar of heavy rain woke me up. Bethany called and told me they'd decided to move the events back an hour to see if the rain would stop. If it didn't, then we'd compete, anyway. But we wouldn't have time to practice beforehand.

Tutu hugged me. "It's okay. You're used to the rain, and so is Sunshine."

I nodded. But a lump in my throat made swallowing my breakfast impossible. Finally, the rain slowed to a drizzle.

Heidi and Liko met me at the stables.

"You nervous?" Liko asked.

"Of course she's nervous," Heidi said with a sniff. "Aren't you?"

"Well . . . yeah," he admitted. "But I'm not about to lose my horse . . . you get it?"

Heidi threw her hands into the air. "You have no idea how to talk to people, do you?"

I ignored them and made a beeline for Sunshine. Bethany had already put the saddle on and was adjusting the stirrups. "Hey," she said. "Liko, your horse is down with your uncle."

"See you both later," he said. He gave me a thumbs-up. "Remember, Starley: You're going to dominate!"

Heidi gave me a quick hug. "You're going to be amazing. I'll see you after, okay?"

I nodded and tried to smile. I listened as Bethany ran through all I needed to do. She helped me mount and then finished adjusting the stirrups.

Bethany pointed. "Head that direction. You'll see Leo, and he'll get you situated."

"You aren't coming with me?" I asked in surprise.

"I'll meet you there. I need to finish a couple of things first." She smiled comfortingly. "It's a straight shot. You'll be fine."

I took my reins and nudged Sunshine forward. There were so many people and horses.

Sunshine skittered sideways when we walked by a loud group of people cheering. "It's okay, girl. Nothing to be scared of."

I kept a firm hand on the reins and kept my voice as soothing as possible. Sunshine quieted, her ears twitching as she listened. She held her head high as she walked through the crowd toward the arena.

Barrel racing was first. This was my first time competing in the barrel-racing event. My stomach skittered like Sunshine did around noise.

I breathed a sigh of relief when I saw Tutu waiting for me at the gate.

"There you are, keiki! I thought you got lost, yeah?"

"I almost did," I said, looking around at the rodeo sprawled out like its own small town. "I didn't know it would be *this* big."

Tutu shook her head and hummed along to the song playing over the loudspeaker. "Hawai'i Pono'i" was one of the first Hawaiian songs I'd ever learned. I wasn't sure if Tutu's singing was meant to soothe Sunshine or me. "You know what I see?" Tutu asked when the song finished.

"What?" I asked, trying to focus on her face.

"I see my brave granddaughter. You can do this,

my girl! You've put in the work. You and Sunshine know each other's thoughts." Tutu reached into her large leather purse. "I have something for you." She handed me a silver pin with a delicate etching of a horse prancing. "Your grandfather gave me this when we first started dating. He loved to watch me ride. Wear this, and you're guaranteed your best ride."

"Thank you, Tutu!" I admired the detail of the horse. It was so lifelike! I pinned it to the front of my shirt and touched the smooth metal lightly.

"I'm proud of you, Starley," Tutu said. "No matter what happens, I'm proud of you. You don't give up. You fight for what you love."

I swallowed and blinked back tears. "Thank you, Tutu."

Leo walked over and took hold of Sunshine's bridle. "Time to go, Starley."

"Love you," Tutu called as we headed to the gate.

The buzzer blared over the speakers surrounding the rodeo grounds. Bethany ran up, breathing heavily. "Sorry I'm late." She double-checked my stirrups and adjusted my grip. "Remember to relax and enjoy this. You've trained hard. You both know what to do."

"I'll try my best," I said, nerves galloping along with my heart.

Bethany smiled. "I know you will."

I sat up straight. "Ready, girl?" I murmured to Sunshine.

I could feel Sunshine's muscles tense. She was getting ready. I gathered the reins in both hands and looked past the gate to the stands. Heidi and Liko waved from the sidelines. "Go get 'em, Starley and Sunshine!" Heidi yelled.

Chapter 23
All or Nothing

My stomach stopped skittering. All I felt was Sunshine. We'd run this same course so many times, it might as well be painted on the back of my eyelids. The crowd's noise quieted.

I closed my eyes and saw the mountains behind Bethany's house. The smell of the jasmine growing next to the barn mixed in with hay and feed. The sounds of chickens, Bethany's dog barking at the wind, and the horses nickering back and forth.

The announcer counted down. When the buzzer sounded, I tapped my heels lightly against Sunshine's side and clicked my tongue. She lunged forward, her entire body focused on navigating the barrels in front of her.

We flew to the first barrel, barely slowing down as we rounded it. Sunshine's neck turned gracefully, her body following. We raced to the next one. I slowed Sunshine down just enough to make the tight turn of the second barrel. One more, and it was time to run full-out to the finish. We rounded the third barrel. I let out my breath as we cleared it. *This is it. All or nothing.*

I held the reins in both hands, my arms straight in front of me, like I could make her go faster if I held them that way. "Go, Sunshine!" I shouted.

Sunshine's hooves pounded the sand. Wind whistled in my ears and whipped my face. I leaned forward, my ʻōkole off the saddle and my weight over Sunshine's neck. I wondered if she knew what was at stake. *Is that why she flew across the arena faster than she's ever run before?*

I heard the crowd cheer. Sunshine's breathing and mine mixed together until they were one. We thundered across the finish line. Sand kicked up all around us as we skidded to a stop. Sunshine snorted and pawed the ground, still wanting to run.

The buzzer sounded like a trumpet, and I knew. I could feel it along my skin and in my heart.

"Good girl," I said. I leaned over and stroked her neck. "You were amazing!"

Bethany held Sunshine as I hopped down. She hugged me tight. "That was your best time!"

Tutu rushed up with Heidi and Liko. They all laughed and took turns hugging me.

I felt lightheaded as we waited for the two

other racers to finish. I recognized the last horse. A beautiful palomino.

I turned to Heidi. “It’s Kristina!”

Kristina was the best barrel racer around. There was no way I was beating her.

Liko frowned. “No worries, Starley. You got this.”

I knew he was just trying to make me feel better. But he didn’t.

Kristina raced around the barrels like lightning, and I held my breath. She walked her horse to the side and waited. I recognized the woman at her side. Maria González.

Tears filled my eyes, turning the arena into a watercolor painting. The announcer’s voice boomed. A loud cheer rolled through the crowd like a wave.

All the air in my lungs whooshed out. I placed both hands on my head and burst into tears.

Chapter 24
Starley and Sunshine

"You won!" Liko shouted. He and Heidi grabbed each other and jumped up and down.

Bethany closed her eyes and sagged in relief. Tutu laughed so loudly, her hat fell off. She hugged me tight while I cried.

I leaned against Sunshine. "You're mine," I whispered. Sunshine's ears waggled back and forth, and she gave a short whinny. It seemed as if she were agreeing.

"Great riding," Kristina said with a pinched mouth.

I smiled. "Thanks. You too."

Maria grabbed Kristina's elbow and hurried her away.

The rest of the day went by in a blur. I won the steer-undecorating event, and Heidi placed fourth. I also won the final race at the end. Liko won his division in calf roping.

After the competitions, Leo took Tutu back to the hotel so she could rest.

"The officials want to know what they should do with the check," Bethany said as she helped me groom Sunshine. "The other winners have already specified."

"Other winners?" I stopped brushing Sunshine's mane and looked up at Bethany.

"Yeah," she said. "The first through fourth place

finishers all split the grand prize."

My stomach dropped. "I have to split the five thousand dollars? I won't have enough to buy Sunshine from Mr. Griffin!"

Bethany frowned at me. "No, Starley. Each event splits five thousand. And since you came in first place for three events, your portion is six thousand dollars."

"Six thousand dollars?" I covered my mouth with both hands. "I'll have money left over! I can buy a new saddle and new boots and—"

"And help your parents with the vet bills," Bethany suggested with a laugh.

A warm feeling started at the tips of my toes and filled me to the top of my head. "Thank you, Bethany. I couldn't have done this without your help."

She nodded. "It was my pleasure."

I went back to brushing Sunshine. I peeked over

at Bethany. "I was wondering about working at your ranch. Do you still need me?"

"You have a job with me for as long as you want it," she said, her eyes never leaving the saddle she was polishing. "I like having you around, Starley. And this pretty girl, too, of course."

"We're a package deal," I said with a happy smile.

Bethany smiled at me. "I wouldn't have it any other way."

~

The announcer's voice boomed over the loudspeakers. "A big aloha to everyone this fine day, and congratulations to the winners in the keiki division. First place is Starley Robinson from the north shore of Oahu with her horse, Sunshine."

The crowd's applause drowned out the beating of my heart. I rode Sunshine forward, and they pinned a bright blue ribbon on her bridle. A tall Hawaiian man handed me the trophy. “Congratulations,” he said as he tipped his giant cowboy hat toward me. He smiled and stepped closer to the microphone. “Can I hear another round of applause for Starley and her horse, Sunshine?”

“Hear that, girl?” I leaned close to her ear. “They’re talking about us.”

Starley and *her* horse, Sunshine. I liked the sound of that.

Don't Miss These Other

American Horse Tales

Books!

Available Now